BABY COMES HOME

BABY COMES HOME

by Debbie Driscoll

illustrated by
Barbara Samuels

Simon & Schuster
Books for Young Readers

Published by Simon & Schuster

New York
London
Toronto
Sydney
Tokyo
Singapore

SIMON & SCHUSTER BOOKS FOR YOUNG READERS
Simon & Schuster Building, Rockefeller Center,
1230 Avenue of the Americas,
New York, New York 10020.
Text copyright © 1993 by Debbie Driscoll.
Illustrations copyright © 1993 by Barbara Samuels.
All rights reserved including the right of
reproduction in whole or in part in any form.
SIMON & SCHUSTER BOOKS FOR YOUNG READERS
is a trademark of Simon & Schuster.
Designed by Lucille Chomowicz.
The text for this book was set in Gill Sans Light.
The illustrations were done in watercolor and
pen and ink.
Manufactured in the United States of America
10 9 8 7 6 5 4 3 2 1
Library of Congress Cataloging-in-Publication Data
Driscoll, Debbie.
Baby comes home/by Debbie Driscoll; illustrated by Barbara Samuels.
Summary: Illustrations and very brief text describe Baby's
activities on the first day home.
[1. Babies—Fiction.]   I. Samuels, Barbara, ill.   II. Title.
PZ7.D7874Bab 1992 [E]—dc20 CIP 91-24114
ISBN 0-671-75540-4

For Paula Jones Gardiner…who
encouraged me to dare to dream,
trust the truth,
live the life,
and learn to dance
– DD

To Nick and Noah, with love
– BS

Hear voices.
Be still.

No one's looking.
Sneak out.

Mama rests.
Stomp away.

Papa cooks.
Spill juice.

Baby naps.
Take blanket.

Baby cries.
Cover ears.

Baby screams.
Pat head.

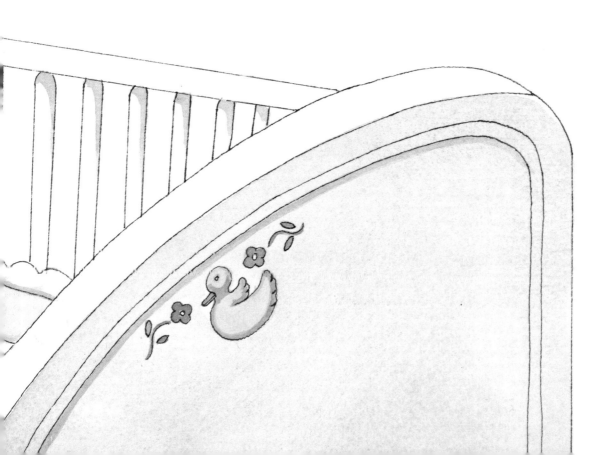

Baby drools.
Make face.

Feet kick.
Jiggle crib.

Touch fingers.
Baby holds.

Wiggle tongue.
Baby looks.

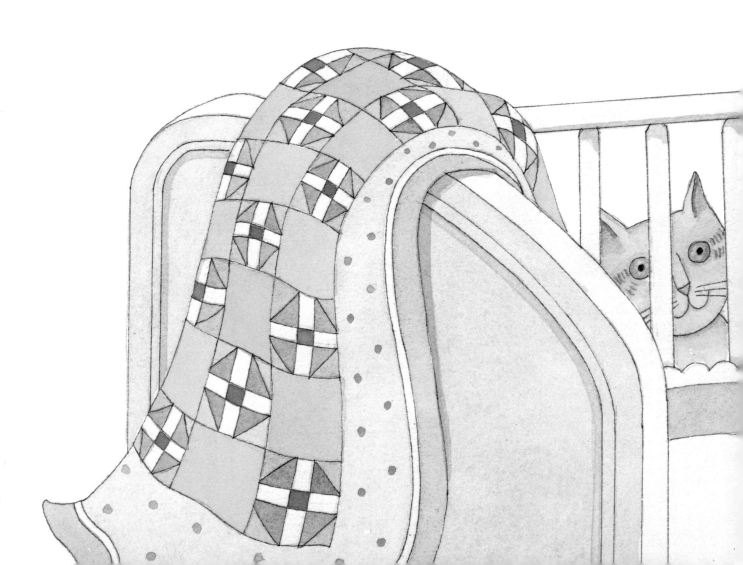

Sing song.
Baby smiles.

Smile back.
Baby's home.